Bugglar Brothers ™

Written by Stephen Cosgrove
Illustrated by Charles Reasoner

READ ALOUD TOPSY-TURVY LIBRARY

H. S. STUTTMAN INC., *Publishers*
Westport, Connecticut 06889

READ ALOUD TOPSY-TURVY® LIBRARY
Published by H. S. STUTTMAN INC.
Westport, Connecticut 06880

© 1988 H. S. Stuttman Inc.
© 1984 Rourke Enterprises, Inc.
© 1983 Price, Stern, Sloan Publishers, Inc.

PRINTED IN THE UNITED STATES OF AMERICA

ISBN 0-87475-600-6

4-26 2P(1340)20-40

As you lay on a summer's day
In a warm and sunny place,
Don't look up into the skies;
Instead, look down
        And squint your eyes.
Squint them both so very tight
That if you look
        With all your might
You'll find the land of
        Morethansmall.
And in this land are buggs,
        that's all.

The farther you drive, walk, crawl or creep down Bugg Street, in the direction of Bugg Bay, the more you notice the neighborhood becoming dilapidated. A lot of the old buildings are abandoned, with their doors and windows boarded up. Dark hats pulled down over their antennae, sneaky-looking buggs skulk and scurry about, looking for something ungood to do...

It was in this really bad section of Bugg-ville that the Bugglar brothers, Barnie and Bernie, lived. Their home was the worst-looking building in the worst part of the worst section of town.

If you ever met them, you would notice that their smiles were a little shifty and that they never looked you straight in the eye. These were bad buggs, Barnie and Bernie, living in a bad part of town.

Whenever Barnie and Bernie would go into respectable shops such as the Buggville Toy Store, the owner would notice that a lot of stuff would end up missing after the brothers had left.

The two of them would slither through the store, and even though all the employees, including the owner, Bugg McSquint, were watching from every nook and cranny, half the store would be missing when the Bugglars left.

Barnie and Bernie would stroll out and appear very nonchalant and casual, until they were out of sight of the store. Then they would break into sneaky snorts of laughter as they inspected their trove of ill-gotten loot.

One day, as they shuffled through Buggville, they spied Snugg, a small happy bugg, looking through the window of the Buggville Toy Store. He was staring so intently at a brand new buggball mitt that he didn't even hear Barnie or Bernie crawl up beside him. "What's up, pal?" they asked, as they sneaked their arms around his shoulders. "Nice looking mitt. Do you play buggball?" They fired off questions so fast that Snugg didn't notice they had stolen his friendship.

"Yup," said Snugg, "That sure is a neat mitt. Someday, if I save up all my money, I'm going to buy one just like it."

"Why not take it now?" said Barnie.

Snugg stopped in his tracks and said, "You don't mean steal it. No way."

"Ahh, Snugg," croaked Bernie, "old McSquint has probably got hundreds of those mitts. He'll never miss just one."

"It's like borrowing," said Barnie. "You don't get in trouble for borrowing."

"Well . . ." said Snugg.

"Come on!" they laughed. "We'll show you how to borrow things."

The rest of the morning the Bugglar brothers took Snugg from store to store as they "borrowed" everything in sight. They borrowed corn, candy, clothes, cameras, and even a canine critter called Carmen from the Buggville Pet Store.

"See!" they gloated, "there's nothing to it. You find something you like, make sure no one's looking, and 'borrow' it."

Snugg wasn't sure, but he liked that buggball mitt and it sure looked easy. Besides, it would take him at least a year to save up the money and the buggball season was just starting.

So they went back to the Buggville Toy Store and, with Bernie and Barnie safely watching from outside, Snugg sauntered in and walked up to a display of the beautiful mitts. He "borrowed" his favorite one, stuffed it under his shirt, and walked right out the door. He hadn't taken more than three steps when the long arm and firm voice of Officer Beadle froze him in his tracks. "Stop, thief!"

The last thing Snugg saw before the tears clouded his vision was the Bugglar brothers running around the corner.

Officer Beadle marched Snugg back into the store and right up to a very angry Bugg McSquint.

"Why, Snugg?" asked Mr. McSquint. "You don't need to steal. If you had wanted the mitt so badly, you could have worked hard to earn it."

"But I didn't mean to steal it," he blubbered. "The Bugglar brothers told me it was more like borrowing."

"Ah, ha," said Officer Beadle. "So, it was the Bugglar brothers who put you up to this caper. Snugg, stealing is stealing, even if you steal a fancy name to call it."

A little too late, Snugg understood.

With head hung low, Snugg led the Buggville police to the hideout of the infamous Bugglar brothers. There, after Barnie and Bernie had stopped crying, they revealed where their ill-gotten gains were hidden.

That very same day Snugg, Barnie and Bernie were taken before the famous judge of Buggville County, Judge Roy Bugg.

After he had heard all the evidence, he looked down at the criminals before him. "Well," he murmured, "I hope you have all learned a valuable lesson."

They all nodded their heads in agreement because just before they had come to court, they had received sound and firm spankings from their parents.

"Normally," the Judge continued, "I'd put you all in jail, but instead I'm going to make the punishment fit the crime."

Snugg and the Bugglar brothers, Barnie and Bernie, gave back all they had stolen. They took the mitt back to the Buggville Toy Store. They gave it all back-but there was more.

From that day forward and for the rest of the year, the three of them, since they were so good at picking up things that didn't belong to them, picked up all the garbage and litter in Buggville Park.

And believe me, they never stole or "borrowed" again.

If you wish to own something and think to steal or borrow, remember the Bugglar brothers and all their grief and sorrow.

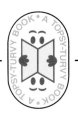

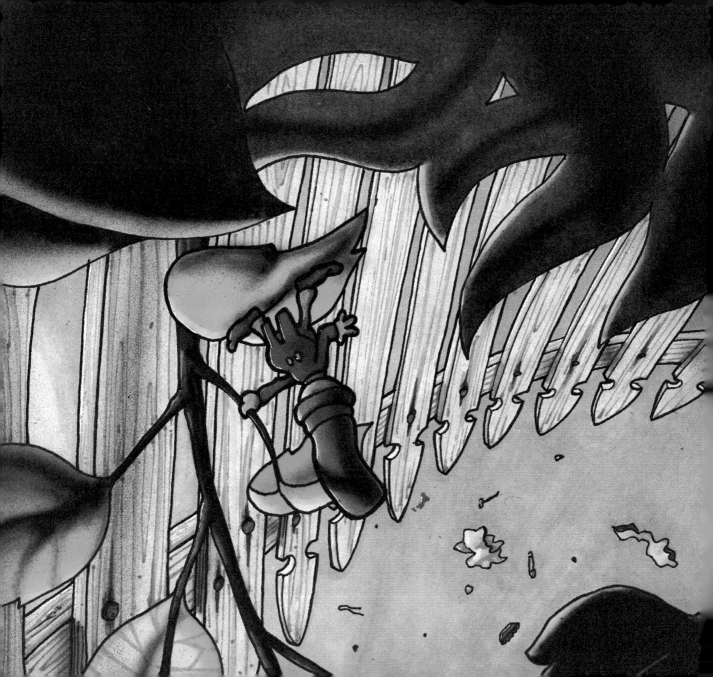

If some junk flies over the fence
And you say, "It makes no sense!"
Maybe it's buggs, you laugh and grin
Maybe . . . but probably it's just the wind.

When all of the garbage was gone, the Mayor waved the flag again to stop the only war in all of bugg history. Tired, they rested in the shade. Once again Morethan-small was spick and span, and neat and shiny. All of the buggs hoped that there would be no more litter wars.

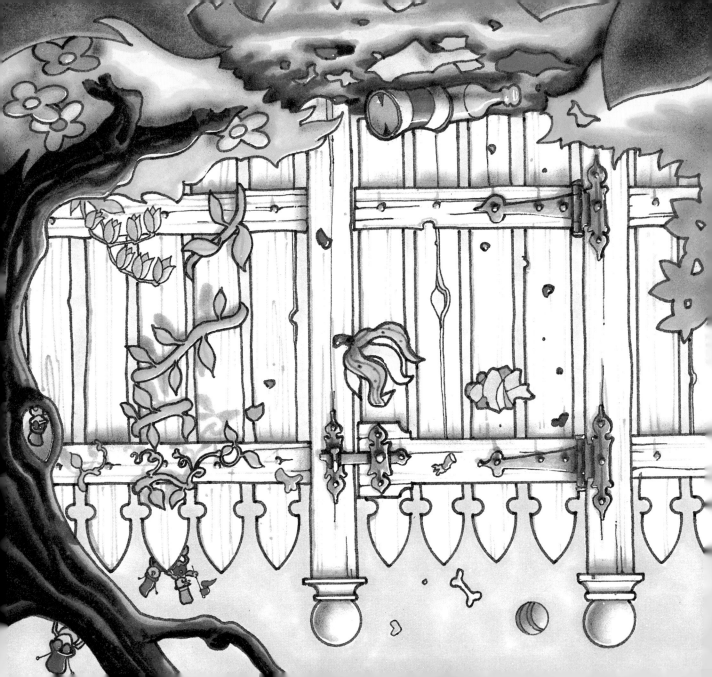

When Mayor Buggwig was sure his tiny army was ready, he waved the Buggville flag. Then, like a great wave crashing on the shore, the garbage and litter whooshed over the fence and landed in the giants' backyard.

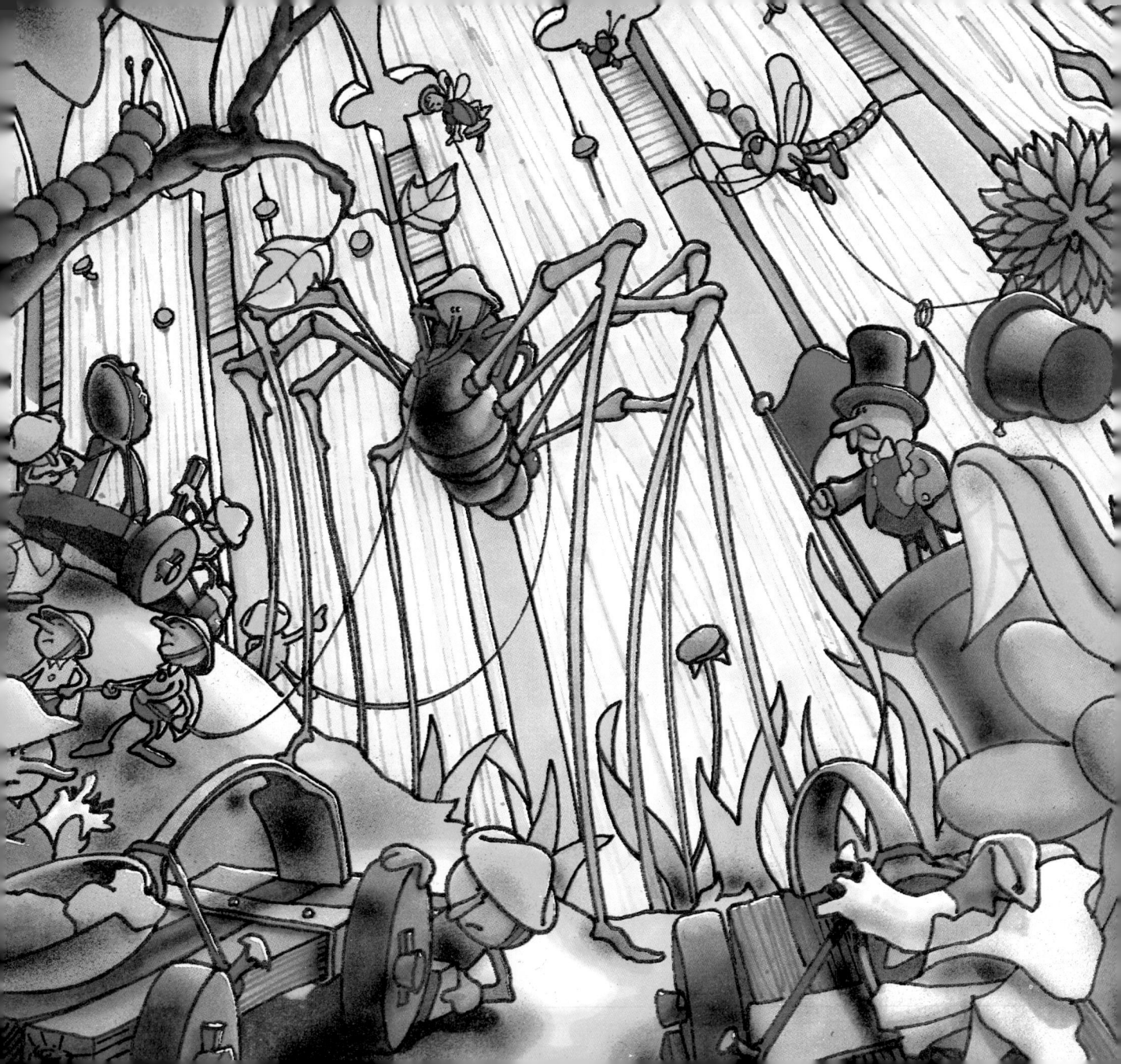

When they reached the fence, the flying buggs went into a holding pattern. The footbuggs lined up and waited for the start of the Great Garbage War.

edge of
fence.

. . . right up to the
the old picket

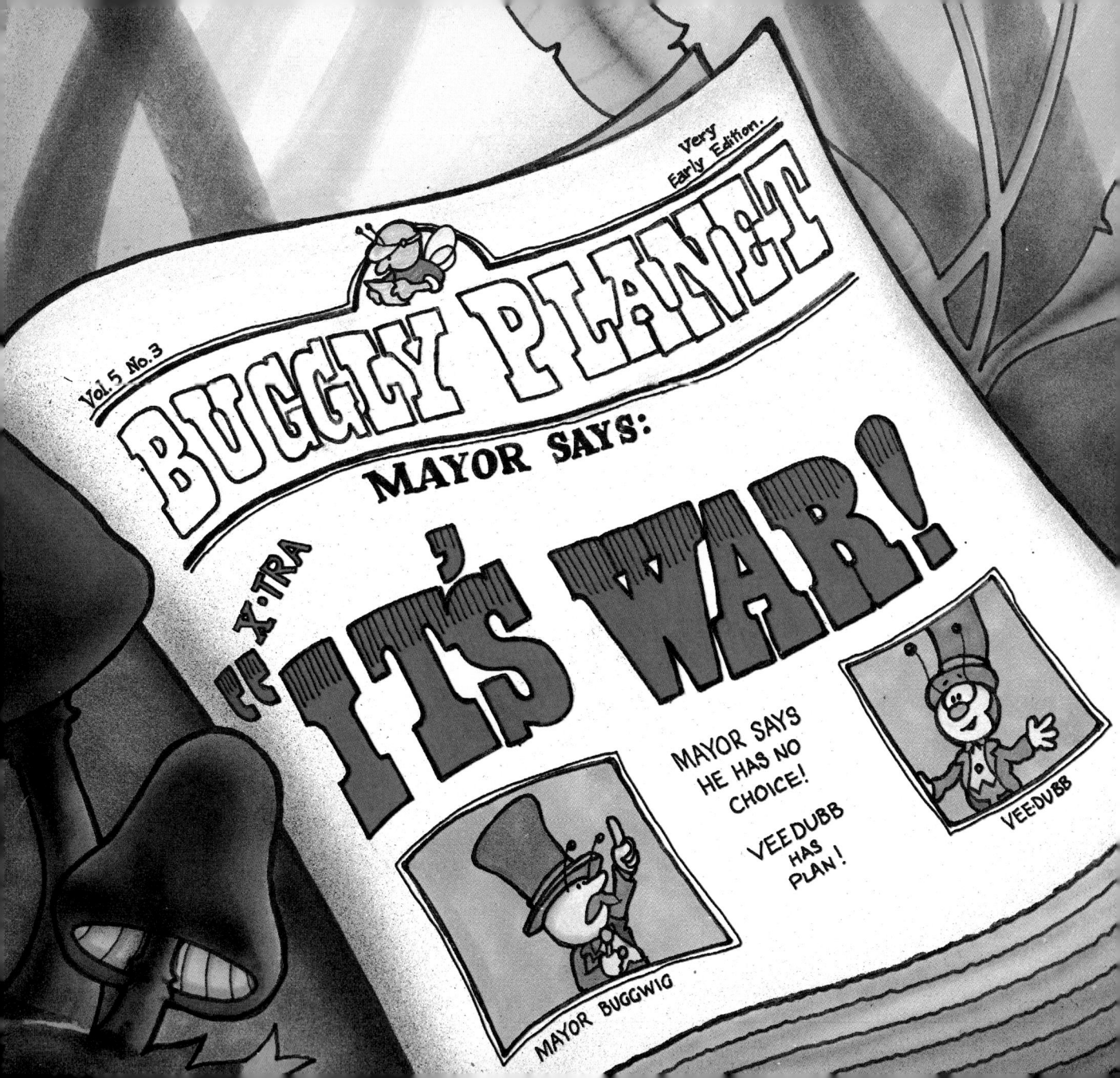

The next day the headlines in the Buggville newpaper declared war on the messy giants. All loyal and patriotic buggs were asked to report to the Armory to be issued garbage disposal weapons.

Soon hundreds of buggs were on the march, pulling catapults and hurlers and slings made from rubber bands. The dragonflies flew in formation, carrying grapples and long lines with hooks on the ends so they could lift the garbage high in the air.

They moved forward as quietly as they could . . .

The humming and buzzing and whirring sounds got louder as the buggs thought. Suddenly Vee-Dubb had an idea. "You know," he said, "the garbage comes from across the fence . . . the big fence, where the giants live. So it must be their garbage. Let's send it back where it came from."

Mayor Buggwig's face lit up. "Yes, yes!" he shouted. "This means war." He smiled a big smile, because politicians always like to talk like that. "War," he said again. "We'll throw the garbage on the giants for a change."

That evening all of the buggs in Buggville met at the City Hall. They jumped and hopped and flitted about, buzzing and humming and whirring. They were all furious, especially Mayor Buggwig.

The Mayor called the meeting to order. "Fellow buggs," he said, "our town is becoming a dump. This litter falling from the sky must stop."

"Yes, yes!" shouted the buggs. "But what shall we do?"

"Ummmm. Hmmmm," said the Mayor. "We must all buggle down and think of something."

But just when the buggs had finally gotten their town cleaned up, it started to pour again. Coffee grounds, broken bottles, old lettuce leaves . . . all came in a huge bombardment.

The buggs were naturally upset. It is unpleasant enough when you have to clean up your own mess, but when you have to clean up someone else's, over and over . . . well, it is enough to make even a bugg really mad.

By the time he got to town, the Buggville fire department and sanitation engineers and all the private citizens were out cleaning up the terrible mess.

One morning, just as he was halfway between his house and the school, Vee-Dubb noticed the leaves fluttering and heard a whistling like the wind before a storm. He started to hide under a leaf, but before he could take a step, it began to pour. It didn't pour rain or sleet or snow. It began to pour garbage. All sorts of junk came falling through the air.

On the outskirts of Buggville, in a house that is a book—or is it a book that is a house?—lives a young bugg named Vee-Dubb.

Every schoolday morning Vee-Dubb is up at seven. He gets his morning newspaper, and at seven forty-five he walks to the Buggville School.

A little north of nowhere and a bit south of your backyard, in a clump of weeds at the foot of a very old tree, is the tiny town of Buggville.

As you lay on a crisp fall day
In a warm and sunny place,
Don't look up into the skies;
Instead, look down
      And squint your eyes.
Squint them both so very tight
That if you look
      With all your might
You'll find the land of
      Morethansmall.
And in this land are buggs,
      that's all.

READ ALOUD TOPSY-TURVY® LIBRARY
Published by H. S. STUTTMAN INC.
Westport, Connecticut 06880

© 1988 H. S. Stuttman Inc.
© 1984 Rourke Enterprises, Inc.
© 1983 Price, Stern, Sloan Publishers, Inc.

4-26 2P(1340)20-40

Vee-Dubb

Written by Stephen Cosgrove
Illustrated by Charles Reasoner

READ ALOUD TOPSY-TURVY LIBRARY

H. S. STUTTMAN INC., *Publishers*
Westport, Connecticut 06889